Meet Boo Boo Kitty!

By Tom Kotay
Drawn by TChuck Garman

Dorrance Publishing Co
585 Alpha Drive
Suite 103
Pittsburgh, PA 15238
Visit our website at *www.dorrancebookstore.com*

ISBN: 978-1-6386-7215-9
eISBN: 978-1-6386-7744-4

Meet Boo Boo Kitty!

By Tom Kotay
Drawn by TChuck Garman

I'm Boo Boo Kitty. I'm a special cat ... can't you tell? I can think and talk and feel things like so many in God's world.

But I'm getting ahead of the story!

I was created on the night of a very bad storm.
Back then, I wondered why the lady made me.

Macey told me that Aunt NeeNee is the lady who made me. I'm a boy cat. It happened on that stormy night in the summer many years ago. Storms don't frighten me, but I don't go out in them because my skin is very sensitive.

Are you afraid of bad weather?

I came to life that first day, but I had so many questions ...

Who am I?
What am I?
Where am I?
Why was I created?

I quickly found out that NeeNee had a husband, TomTom, and they had a dog and a cat. None of them bothered much with me. I was very delicate at an early age. They all seemed to like me, but I didn't know why.

NeeNee said that I was soon leaving and going to a new home. What's a home, I thought? I said to myself that I'm a smart cat. I'll figure out this home-business before too long. But I also had this funny stomach, like butterflies were flying around inside me.

I guess I was scared.

Have you ever been scared?

NeeNee said that I was going to live with Macey and her parents in their home.

That made me feel a little better, but remember, I'm a cat so I am CURIOUS.

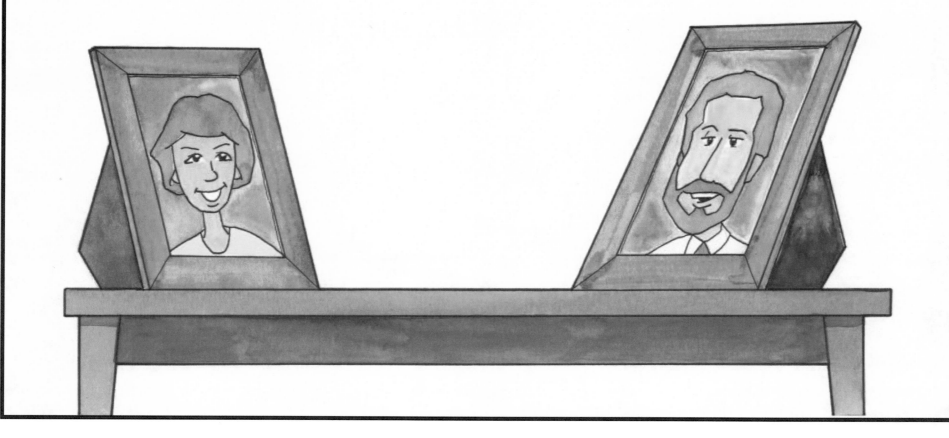

And I still didn't know what a home was all about.

Well, the day finally came, and NeeNee, TomTom, and I got into their car for the journey to Macey's home.

As we left the driveway, I finally figured out what a home is ... it's a place where people live. How excited I was to learn new things!

NeeNee said we were just about there as we turned the corner from one street to another. But my head was still spinning from all that I had seen so far! Things that I didn't understand back then, but now I do.

Traffic lights, a train, tall buildings, a hospital, farm fields, pigs and horses and cows, and so much more ... they all made me think about how wonderful this place was.

I was surprised when we got there ... to Macey's home. It didn't look like NeeNee and TomTom's home.

It had a very big yard and there was a boy dog outside with Macey, her mother, and her father. They were playing and I wanted to join in!

Macey was very small back then, but when she first saw me, I knew it was love at first sight, even though I had yet to figure out what love was all about. She hugged me, and I felt all warm inside.

I felt safe.

I now know that NeeNee made me to love Macey.

Well, as you can imagine, I was a hit ... I was a cute and cuddly cat! Don't you agree? Everyone loved me and I loved them! I now know that love is something very special that we all need to cherish. It's about caring for and being concerned about others.

I have so much more to tell you about my life, our adventures as a family and what I've learned along the way, but those stories are for another time.

Because I'm such a CURIOUS cat, I'd like to see what your home and family look like. I've drawn this picture of my family and where we currently live north of Pittsburgh. On the opposite page, please draw a picture of your home and family.

It's OKAY if someone helps you draw and color your picture.

BOO BOO KITTY'S CORNER

When you are finished, you can upload your picture
to BooBooKittyBooks.com. I'd love to show it off!

Macey & Boo Boo, 1989

Note from the author: In the Bible we read,
"And now these three things remain: faith, hope and love.
But the greatest of these is love."
1 Corinthians 13:13

Watch for Boo Boo Kitty's next outing coming soon!

"The Early Adventures of Boo Boo Kitty!"

Go to BooBooKittyBooks.com for information and updates.

Thanks for reading!

CPSIA information can be obtained
at www.ICGtesting.com
Printed in the USA
BVRC100946200222
628847BV00003B/9